Chaos in Utter Silence

A Collection of Prose & Poetry

LARAIB ZAKIR

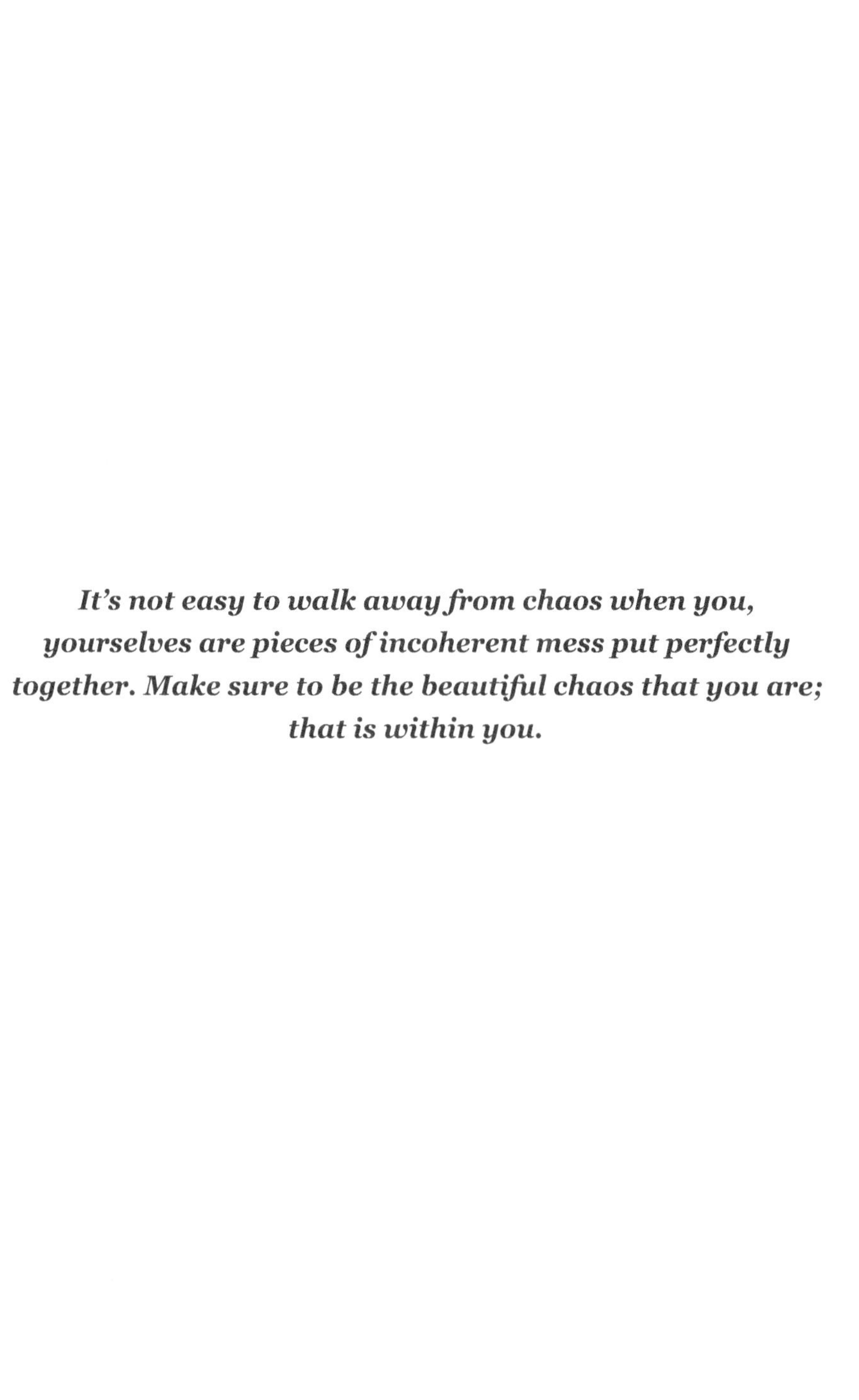

It's not easy to walk away from chaos when you, yourselves are pieces of incoherent mess put perfectly together. Make sure to be the beautiful chaos that you are; that is within you.

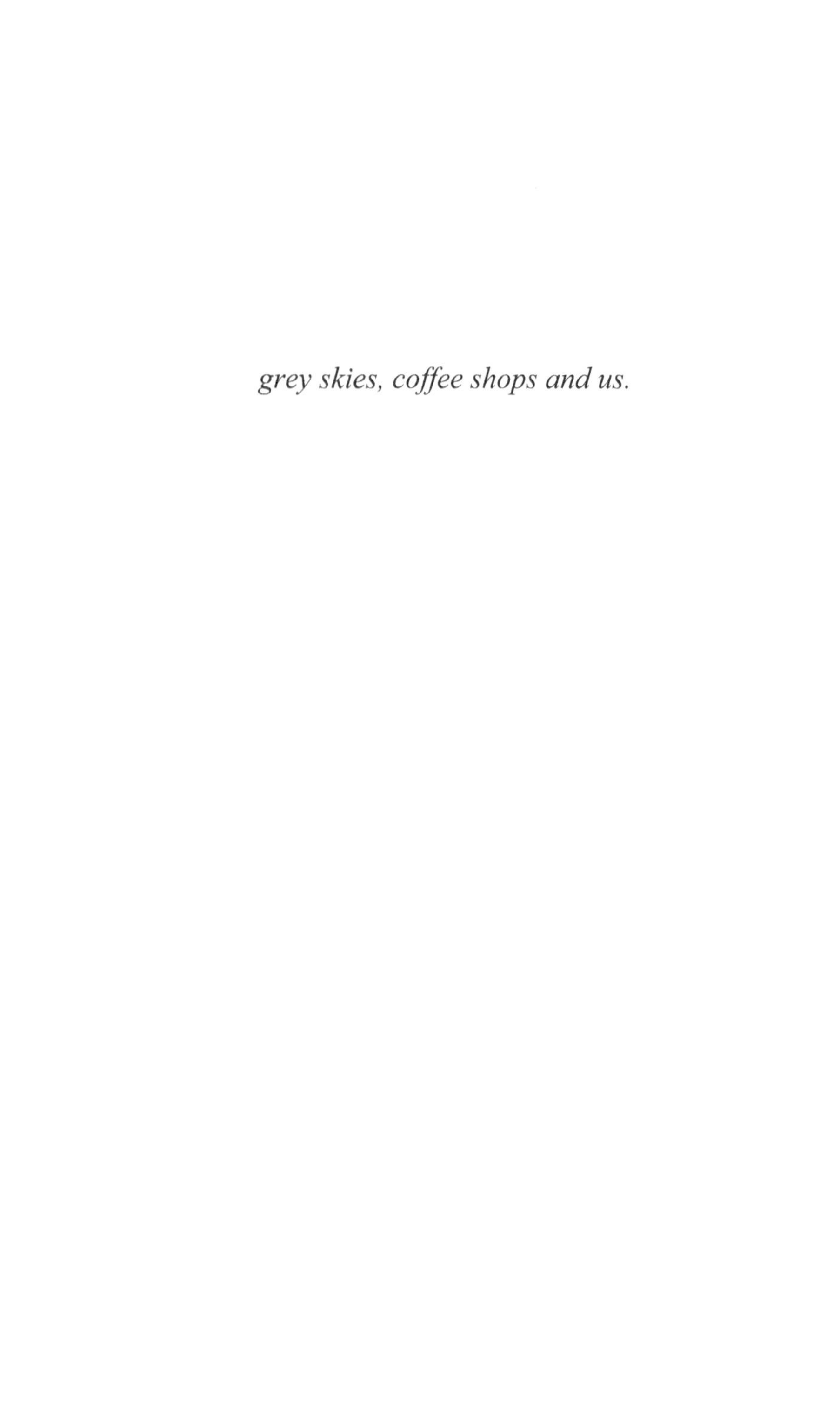

grey skies, coffee shops and us.

CONTENTS

Prose

Poetry

Prose

Shattered

The floor was strewn with smithereens of the glass, which had fallen lovingly from her hand. It seemed so familiar. The pieces that lay contended, didn't cease to reflect. Reflect on her. Reflect in her fading grey irises. Closing her eyes for a moment, taking a deep breath, trying to hush down the rapidly beating heart, pushing back the stray auburn strands of hair behind her ears and calming the strains on her forehead, she steadily lifted the velvety maroon quilt. Straightening her strained neck to sit up, she struggled with several bone-crushing aches at a single moment. It was hard to see if any of her parts was spared from the agony she was going through.

The simmering crystal fragments had certainly found a grave within her.

Dystopia

It was tiresome to even think about walking barefoot on the vast, barren and repulsive path that lay ahead. It waited. It seemed as if it had always wanted to crucify her soul with every step that she took. Her existence was a burden. The eerie silence was deafening. She had to choose between a stagnant death and a death that was painful yet exhilarating; death that never witnessed her and a death that awaited her presence. The wind breathed life into her creamy hair; they swayed across her emaciated face. It was becoming bitter; everything was becoming bitter, the cold, and the agony. She could feel the stinging cold deep into her bones, making her ache inexhaustibly.

Crumble Again

It takes nothing but little pieces to crumble now and then. For once, in a long while, you might feel whole. But fortunately, you know that you will crumble again.

Apathy

But then, who's there to tell me to pick the shambles of lethargy and walk ahead, to wake up from the long slumbers that always feel like never enough, and to gather the ruins of weakened bones and sticks, and set them in a place, far away?

Laraib Zakir

The Name. The Thought. The Fear

"Is there no way out of the mind?"
- Sylvia Plath

The Name (1/3)

You try to get rid of that name in your head and it gets stuck in your throat. Stubborn, it stays there. Your efforts to swallow it into oblivion go in vain and your attempts to exhale it out of your existence seem futile. It gets hold of you; a firm footing within. You feel it running through your veins. You begin to utter it, bit by bit, usually in silence. You utter it while walking, while travelling somewhere far. Just before you sleep and the moment you wake up, you find it on the tip of your tongue. For long, it has found its home in you. You carry that name, you always do. Until one day, you decide to numb it. Because you can no longer hold it inside anymore.

The Name. The Thought. The Fear

The Thought (2/3)

You will always be on my mind, won't you? I'll wake up early in the morning and think that you are probably still sleeping; I'll cross a road and wonder whether you have ever been on that road too. It will rain and I'll think if you love it as much as I do. If I go to eat at any place, the thought of you being over there will come to me and what you would have liked on the menu. The moment I'm extremely happy, the moment I am deeply saddened, the moment I need to tell something to someone, it is you, who comes to my mind. The thought of you never leaves. Does it?

Laraib Zakir

The Name. The Thought. The Fear

The Fear (3/3)

And with the name, with the thought, comes the fear, inevitably and unapologetically. Come to think of it. We know that it was always, always there. Wasn't it? With its fingers gripping the heart, it drains the little melodies out of it and places the broken pieces of melancholy inside, carefully so, to not let them escape. With its feet dipped in cold water in a winter night and a full moon, it sends paralysing chills down the spine. More than often, the heart skips a beat because of this fear which lives in the conscience, spreading its web around the entire existence and sometimes lingers through the veins, just to remind that it is what is keeping us alive, for now. How immaculately the fear resides in us when it knows what we fear is not even ours. It's just the name and numerous thoughts that we carry.

and in all this, amongst uttering the name to brushing off the thoughts which relentlessly come back to see the fear winning and taking its toll, I wonder, if ever, you could know that it is you.

Laraib Zakir

Bitterness

The bitter cold seeps into her feeble bones. It spreads like poison, slowly yet painfully. The dreadfulness, the restlessness and gloominess; all come at once. It strikes so hard that it benumbs the soul. The night is so dark and the day is so bleak. Her thoughts are being clouded by thunderstorms. It's that time when she fails to comprehend anything around her, when everything blurs out, when she falls through piercing webs of grief that occupy her in her sleep.

Sheer Happiness

Flipping to the last page of the novel, she clenches the oversized sweater up to her palms. She re-reads the last lines. How perfect was the ending! She puts the novel aside and picks up another favourite; coffee. The mildly dark colour complements the winter. The steam that rises from the mug is incredibly comforting. The raindrops slither along the window as she childishly traces them with her finger. A tranquil blanket wraps her in its warmth as she relishes in the rain that pours rhythmically outside.

Laraib Zakir

Late November

(1/3)

During the last days of November when divine melancholy blends into the crimson horizons, she waits for the dawn and dusk, simultaneously. Draped in a warm, camel-coloured cashmere shawl, she treads along the pavements that are strewn with lifeless yet crisp leaves. Just like she turns the pages of her poetry, the leaves turn their way towards her. The whirling red, the sea of purple, the burned orange and the perplexed ombre; all finding their ways through the cobbled streets and concrete houses, through shimmering lampposts and dark alleys.

It all begins when a light breeze, (the smallest degree of light) sways the fragile leaves off the branches and it seems as if it is raining leaves— a beautiful sight! With every breeze, a pond of leaves twirls themselves into a graveyard— an inviting one! A tombstone of scarlet, saffron and russet sets ablaze the silhouettes of solitudes to spread like a forest fire never to be extinguished.

Late November

(2/3)

And just when it's time to drink coffee, it's as if the caffeine has settled and drenched down the veins, where once rushed stardust. The bitterness of coffee takes over the thoughts.

And in the moments of bleakness, she thinks to herself of all that has left, that could be hers at the moment, the way things could have been different, different as in not better but just different. She thinks to herself whether she will be able to name it ever or will it always reside in abstractness, in muses that are scattered here and there, in the pressed leaves inside a book's page, or in those unsettled, inconvenient and most of all, incomplete conversations. There's this cartilage of so much left unsaid, so much that was never initiated, of regrets asking certain questions, and of regrets never asking some.

The cascade of people passes by, but she stays oblivious to all that is and remains in what her mind lingers on, what her heart murmurs and where the nothingness takes her.

Late November

(3/3)

At times, the air smells of cider and at times, it smells of certainty overtaken by confusion.

Mist drips steadily on the parchment which then starts to reek of stained anticipations, tainted mornings and tattered writings.

She looks up at the sky more often than she usually does, in an attempt to find relief. Amidst the swirling twilights, it's certainly known to her that it's never the same for everyone.

The late November, she whispers— when fall and winter together weave their magic with a pinch of blood-red, a dash of amber and a drop of brunette in a puff of an icy dewy drop.

Sleeplessness

Tonight, and a few nights that have passed by and the many nights that are to come, I feel a knot at the back of my throat. It's a friable string vulnerably tied to a stone that weighs over my heart.

Each night, I close my eyes in hope that in the morning, as I wake up, the heaviness would lighten, the piercing stone would crumble to dust. But each morning, it doesn't. What weighed at night is heavier now. The dense pain cloaks all over. I faintly live with it as it continues to weigh my breathing down.

But…Sleep.

As the eyes try to contemplate over the whirling concerns of the demented day, there is a little seizing moment at the forehead that pleads to let it all go for now. The pleats at the forehead lighten themselves. The heart, already tired, has surrendered from all that befalls.

A calm settles.

And with that, the eyes faintly blink for the last time, the eyelashes kiss an earnest goodbye to the draining hazel irises.

The night prevails in serenity for someone who dreams of a conflicting, comforting and beautiful chaos in complete silence.

Laraib Zakir

The Creases of Her Hands

(1/6)

Walking towards the collapsed constellations, she halted where silver dust motes shimmered, feline yet chaotic. The entire hallway, engulfed by shattered pieces of mirror, lay mercilessly for her to walk on.

Making her way towards one of the fragmented pieces, she placed the lower side of her hand at the edge to engrave its touch into her skin; it sunk deep into her hand as if it were mesmerizing. There, in its reflection, she saw stardust dancing in the cosmic fields of golden sunflowers, swaying with winds, healing to the tunes of sun-kissed leaves. She let her fingers slide through the mirror, the creases of her hands taking in the aura. But then, the stardust turned into ashes, the previously harmless surface cut through the lower end and crimson dripped, drabbing the peace out of the rusty edges and replacing them with patched burning infernos. Heaped into swirls of ashes, the branches crept up and twined around the veins of her wrist, strangled the life out and left it discoloured.

Faded, she took a few steps back. Ashes— all she could remember were the tawny ashes at the dusk, tangled in her thoughts.

Laraib Zakir

The Creases of Her Hands

(2/6)

Caught by another vulnerable glint, this wreckage of mirror reeked of serenity as she placed herself near. Moonlit, dabbed in diamonds and twinkling with a hundred stars, it lulled the creases of her hands towards it and just by the moment she complied with the starry night, it crashed itself and vanished into a black hole. Engulfed by a hundred galaxies; the thunders churning with the exit and the lightening snivelling with what was left after the havoc. The entire surface was trembling fearlessly as it had scratched off some lines from her hands. Where once ran Milky Way, now stood barren ruins. She clenched her fist slowly and placed it near her heart, near the relics. "Night!" It said as it gleamed down at the mauve sky— crumbling and settling itself in her eyes.

The Creases of Her Hands

(3/6)

Scented with numerous flowerbeds, she chose to walk her hands among the ones with scarlet roses. Soaked in melancholy, they resembled the creases of her hands. Her hands, now withered, devotedly, from left to right of the frame, lightly stroked the sombre petals. Tinted by her touch, they looked up and there she was, sliding herself halfway through the thorns. Pricked by one of those, it quenched its thirst from the wine that trickled from the tip of her finger. Draped in cerise, she chose to escape with the fragrance of roses, her fingers tiringly seeking leave, her nails ticking off the restlessness that throbbed within the skin. Dripping out of the satin mahogany sky, she saw the clouds being sliced out of the pier-glass.

Laraib Zakir

The Creases of Her Hands

(4/6)

She then dragged the creases on her hands to another fragmented crystal mirror; its sides polished with metal. Stunning, it stood eluded from the skies and rested itself among the debris of miserable prison cells. Unlike many others, it clearly showed her reflection— just her. Not being able to see anything beyond her, she paused where she saw a colliding war among hues of grey, light green and hazelnut, all inside her eyes. Swirling, twirling and weaving, they danced off under the night sky. She lifted her finger to be placed amongst the war and saw the stars rearranging themselves in the form of a rib cage, and from therein emerged a heart, with its beats fading into oblivion. She felt a sharp pain piercing into her ribs, sucking the air out of her lungs, plunging the whispers out of the gut and tying knots in her throat. Fractured was the mirror and now, her bones. The creases of her hands drowned into the lost apartments of old graveyards.

The Creases of Her Hands

(5/6)

Fuming with potions of frailty, this piece stroked long strands of her light chestnut hair. It enchanted itself and her onto a rooftop, subsiding into the dark emerald skies. Sheer silence prevailed. Faraway, in a distant street someone burned and puffed the last of their cigarette, ripping it off the sight and brewing the last of its fireworks under the tattered sole of their shoe. But, even long after it was gone, the smoke hazed up in the sky, disappeared into thin air and soaked away the blurred tears into the thick bricked walls. Heaving under the weight of pungent cries that came from afar, her hands climbed down to the windows which creaked to let in and out the wind. The cold breeze murmured a secret into the creases of her hands which now stood still even after the to-and-fro of all that was outside. Numbed by the secret, she was now held hostage by the crumbling dust that only resonated with rumours and which trailed off with maroon moonlight.

Laraib Zakir

The Creases of Her Hands

(6/6)

She moved onto another piece, it glistened with misery. She placed the very same delicate fingers on it. From therein, emerged piles of unkempt papers, scattered all over. Agonised by the familiarity, she sifted through them. Her hands trembling yet working through them. They were all the dead poetries she had written. The words whirled and suffocated her vision; some were burnt, some were cut off and some were there where she expected them to be— lingering in the deepest, grief-stricken dungeons of her heart. Inscribed with sanctity, she felt sharp daggers being stabbed at the pale fingers as they slithered through those words. Paper cuts, numerous of them scraped off the little flesh that was left now. The creases of her hands inhaled the very essence of each word that the poetries hummed with. Drenched in the revered fragrance of ache and drunk on drizzling cold rain, it infused into her bones.

Chaos In Utter Silence

Contrary to what should have been, she felt tranquillity wrapping its warm wings around her, putting her to sweet sleep.

The very words, lost somewhere, written by her, finally calmed the creases on her hands.

Words

The words slip away before being uttered. Tied to the voids, they whirl in hollowness that consumes them. Time fades, and the words; they stand just right there. They walk past where they had to be uttered, turn around to see if they could still be uttered, but then just as they near, they numb themselves. Sealed, the words haunt back but never do they utter.

Yourself

Always hold yourselves close to yourselves. Don't give away too much of yourself to anyone. Nobody cares for what is not theirs. You will find the scattered pieces that you gave away, vanishing. Never to find their way back to you.

Laraib Zakir

Airport

One day, maybe, at 5 in the morning, I'll write a letter to you—while sitting inside the dimly lit airport lounge. Rain pouring incessantly against the glass walls.

My hands trembling at the thought of you. Had I been in front of you, how feeble my voice would have sounded, how shaken my words would have been. How, instead of my hands, the incomplete phrases would have trembled. Everything that I said, would probably fade away in the downpour. My eyes, dull and sunken by this time would beg to shut themselves tightly. I don't know whether to regret or not, that you won't be beside me by then.

From afar, I'll wonder why the runway is so serene when it is I who should have been. I'll get up at the sudden announcements and tread lightly towards the 'Departures' terminal, nudging the suitcase behind me.

Till then, would I have finished writing to you? Will I crumble the paper and throw it in the air so that it lands at the airport's carousel, so that it stays in a place where I left? Or somehow, I'll have that letter sealed in melancholy reach you?

I don't know if you really like to read in general, but the fact that my handwriting isn't better than yours, I'll want to gulp down the paper in silent sobs, wishing that you could have written a hand note to me for once, but oh, how can I forget that we barely talked, or it was I who was always reluctant. But still, a handwritten note from you, even with a line or two, would have been an elixir for me and the nostalgia which has now begun to settle in. I'll confess in my letter, how I loved the flow of your handwriting.

I'll probably hastily stuff it into my pocket as I look for my seat in the airplane and sit by the window with a sigh of short-lived relief— that my legs have carried me up till here without looking back for once. But my mind is still in the place where you are.

All I wish is that as the plane takes off, my memories of you become distant and hazy. But maybe, at the back of my head, I know, that they won't.

Forever

How sacredly we let our thoughts torment us with the notion that it won't last forever, whatever that we want. Whatever that could have been. Whatever that is, is just for mere hours per day, mere days per month, and mere months in a year.

Trials

But some trials are there to persist. You could sense them coming. Like seasons, you cannot undo their arrival. The anxiety, too, at all times is consistent with those trials. You start reliving the last time and wonder how you came out of it. And all you can do is pray; wish you come out of it this time, too.

Laraib Zakir

Prison

I see you vanish into thin air. Oh, but were you even here or my mind is still lingering in the demise of its sanity?

Here, I don't have a picture of you framed in delicate glass to run my hurting fingers across, to dust it off, to see your face reveal from behind.

The four tall walls are as cold as the floor, numb yet distressed. Do they turn into the person who comes to live with them? The bare wooden table in the right corner holds an empty cup, stained with coffee marks. When did I have the last sip? I guess, we barely accept the last of things to actually last. Anguish engulfs the hinges, I don't know which way to stroll, which way will be more kind to my flaking feet. The ankles creak at the thought of you and me, walking together.

This place is blatantly becoming unwelcoming as each day passes. All the bread has crumbled and is stale now. The scartings have rusted off. The smell of paint has been reduced to debris. Fatigued cemeteries would certainly resemble this place.

I sit aloof, trying to ward off the rumours that I live in a void; my hands entangled in my hair, my fingers pressing against my head. It has been an eternity since I last cried. The eyes have dried up by now. They hold no more tears; all they hold is stubbornness and grieving graveyards. I am afraid that my remembrance might get scarred here.

This prison doesn't hold me alone, it has the luggage of unspent days— our unspent days. And I am certainly the one to carry it alone. I see, it is I who has been caged, who has willingly refused to open another door, who has declined the sunlight from barging in, and kept every curtain tightly shut to its core. I remember hammering nails on the sides of them, so they wouldn't flutter with a breeze of the wind. I don't want any of that.

But in all this, do you see what I want?

Laraib Zakir

Monotony

Fainting dawn and muffled alarm wake me up. Time to bid farewell to the long-gone night and its fallen conspiracies.

The curtains give way to sanity. I disentangle myself from the duvet and meekly open the side table drawer. There, I had placed reasoning last night and now it's out to embrace me. Sitting in the middle of the bed, legs hanging down; my feet, an inch away from touching the floor, I let contemplations dissolve inside me for they sleep under my bed.

Walking towards the mirror, the apprehensions come off the reflections to make their way and settle inside of me. I comb my hair, with awareness separating the strands and intuition braiding them for the day. The wardrobe opens its doors for me to pour all my thunders in it and sets forth gentleness to wear.

I pick up the etiquettes from the dressing table and put them away in my bag to carry. Prudence whispers in my ears from afar— now close. The perfume clouds me with incisiveness and leaves scented keenness on my clavicle.

I rhythmically hum my way towards the kitchen and brew coffee full of wit. It tastes of sharpness and judgement. The roasted garlic bread smells of intellect, topped with extra comprehension.

It's time to leave for monotony and later return to madness.

Laraib Zakir

Quieter

I have become quieter, more than I previously was.

But no, if you ever see me, know that the thoughts would be at

work— creating havoc and residing within the chaos.

I have become quieter because the words that came out were never

enough, never understood, and merely listened to. I have become

quieter because one day, it is this silence, I will bury myself in.

Suitcase

She's been lying in there. Crouched, one arm folded around the knees, the other dangling lifelessly; perhaps resting on the brink of the opened suitcase. The calendars from far-flung years come to her and speak of the wasted days and the lost nights.

She remembers the time when a jar filled with reveries slipped from her hands and the musings vanished into thick smoke which reeked of forgetful ashes. She murmurs a line or two from her favourite poetry books. Maybe she had picked up the few fragmented lines from beneath her feet that were covered in blood, with crystals of jar engraved sparsely in her cadaverous skin. Some of the words, by then, were quivering at the thought of clogging at the mere thoughts that somehow kept her alive.

Someone was screaming from afar, maybe the wolves were howling at the full moon or the fireflies were finally caught to be extinguished in one go. Strangely enough, the suitcase, immersed in silence, remained deceitful of what was happening elsewhere because she wanted it to be so. A false cry, she would hush it away. The stillness in the air invoked mercy from her stifled screams.

A newspaper inscribed in pitch-black pungent ink and wrapped in forlorn eulogy emanates from a busy city's stand. It begins to talk of hustle and bustle at the cacophonous road, but then halts at the news of a death— death of someone known to an unknown nostalgia. Brimming with distress, it asks the winds to rip it into pieces, burn them and set them away in a cemetery of drained emotions.

Art

And maybe that's how art is like, you slit golden skies and it rains crimson; dark and profound. Moon-dust and stardust collide to glitter their way down to your throat, dissolving in an eternity. You breathe against mirrors painted with catastrophic tints and sullen epiphanies. Your heads rest on pillows filled with abstract dreams and punctilious nightmares. Several times, does the entire world come crashing down, but you, you pick up the wrecked remains of desolate numbness and piece together a mosaic of fallen constellations. You wear poetry in your eyes, written in grey against the hazel silhouettes. Mist entwines your fingers until it rains and you run into an old building to peek from the cracked walls and dangling chandeliers. You turn several pages in a day— to write, read, paint, sketch, or maybe to just blankly stare at them. You tend to create everything out of nothing, on days drained of life and on days bursting with life. The night candle flickers with tales that trickle down the cauldron of unkempt proses. You splash pastels across the canvas and make yourself a midnight pasta, guilty of torrential cheese that tops it. And maybe that's how art is like— a comforting sanctuary.

Too Early to Leave

Tonight, I feel as if winter is leaving. I ask if it's too early and it whispers with such tranquillity that melancholy settles all over me. With it, it will take away this tinge of cold that the wind carries; it will take away the rustling of the few leaves left on the trees; it will take away the flickering lamp posts covered in dew; it will take away the dark grey skies. I wouldn't have the long sleeves of a sweater to clutch on; I wouldn't warm my hands from the coffee mug anymore; I wouldn't wipe off the windows to see outside. I would no more curl myself inside the blankets. I would no more be sitting by the fireplace, a book in my hand, my thoughts drifting somewhere else. There will be no sound of the ticking of the clock; there will be no sound of twigs cracking in the yard. But there's this winter that resides within me and how grateful I am for it. The cold has enveloped my heart so well, the briskness of the winter evenings creeps up in my veins and the blood congeals to form castles of the dark dungeons of my thoughts. The eyes change colour from green to grey and back to hazelnut, just the way winter arrives and leaves. But in all this, there is a realization; I, too, carry a winter within me at all times.

Poetry

Laraib Zakir

Too Early to Leave

Until the first cold breeze of next winter passes through the open doors.

Until the hallways, the alleys, the pavements soak the bitterness it brings.

Until the silence of all the crowded places haunts me back to the cosy bedroom, the late mornings, and the early evenings.

Until I see the flickering flames of candle swaying to the tunes of winter melodies.

Until I drape myself in cashmere shawls.

Until I sip Kashmiri chai.

Until I drain myself to the point that as I fall into oblivion, winter opens its feathery wings wide open and I lay upon it, waiting for the morning table to be dressed in ginger tea and garlic bread or sweet cake-rusk and warm cheese-omelette.

Until I look up at the sky and find it turning maroon, until I can touch the velvety clouds, until the rain that comes down ferments into vanilla essence.

Until I make myself munch on pistachios, walnuts, resins, cashew nuts, and almonds without being guilty.

Until next winter,

I hope the next time, it lasts longer.

Non-Conformity

And what do you

do of the

non-conformity

that invades

from within?

Somehow, we all are flawed, tragically yet beautifully.

To the Waves

I knew I was walking towards you.
But why?
No, I didn't know that.
It was just that you were there and I had to come to you.
No, I couldn't see you,
I wouldn't be able to,
till the morning.
But, I wanted to listen to you,
to walk in secrecy to you.
I could see the moon,
nearing you
just as I was.
Did you say something to it?
It was pulling you towards itself.
Your thunders
were so calming,
only because I find
serenity in everything fierce.
It was utterly dark,
the starry night enveloped us together
in solitude.
I loved how with every little step,
we were closer.

Laraib Zakir

It was that,
without seeing you,
I could feel the passageways that you took,
where you turned,
where you slowed down
and just how you knew
that I was there.

62

Anxiety

It all starts
and ends
where, instead of you
seeping in anxiety,
anxiety seeps you in.

Isn't it beautiful? To fade away.

Fall

The eyes,
they still search
for the sky
draped in silver-grey.
The feet,
they still want
to walk on the
curled-up leaves,
to hear them crunch underneath
maybe one last time.
The wind,
with its little ache of tingling cold,
I somehow want it back.
I have a heart
that clings on to fall.
Fall forever.

Laraib Zakir

That day

That day when our eyes met
out of nowhere,
the entire world came crashing down.
Averting them each time
repeatedly,
I couldn't keep a count of those accidental encounters.

Moon

It is the moon
that drips into an hourglass,
cutting into phases,
leaving old ridges
callously.

—an eclipse coffins our union.

I turn the mundane into mayhem.

Someday…

I once scribbled:

'Maybe, someday I'll write about you too.'

But guess what?

Look at this entire mess now.

I have written you a hundred times over

in crumpled paper balls,

under the wrinkled eyes,

at the back of my mind,

beneath the still sighs.

I always wanted to write about you

when the strings of my heart would have discorded off from yours,

when we no longer would have something to talk about,

when you would have gone too far.

But now, look at this entire mess.

Atrocities

The fences were too high,
So were the atrocities.

All this time...

I looked for you in the autumn trees;
Between the lifeless leaves and rustling winds.
But you were not there.

I looked for you amidst the corroded brick walls;
Amongst the stale smell and dingy ridges.
But you were not there.

I looked for you from behind the smudged windows;
Beyond the shattered glass and sinking reflections.
But you were not there.

I looked for you amongst the clouded skies;
In the midst of trembling thunders and bewildered lightning.
But you were not there.

Because all this time, you were never there.

Laraib Zakir

Tired

Even after getting tired,
we still,
out of nowhere,
want it to be all right.

Even if it can't.
But still.

You never know what's killing someone from the inside.

Laraib Zakir

I'll wait

Maybe holding on is tiring,
excruciatingly draining of what is left.
It's a little melancholy that goes a long way,
something that withers you away.
Although wilted, you still want it to stay.

That is why.
after waiting for so long
The mind betrays the heart,
heart that yearns to cling on
For a little longer.

But how long is that little longer?
It's too farfetched ever to come back.
Infinitely fabricated to ever become true
And too abstract, even to exist.
Comes the brittle answer.

The damage is what
I wish to reverse
All I now want, is the life
before I met you.

Chaos In Utter Silence

The once strong belief starts to fade away
in a room flickering with doubts.
The fainted arguments
gradually die, over and over again
Until they are finally buried.

Taking your name for the last time
the heart skips a beat
A calm then settles
and that is when I ask you
What have I been waiting for, this long?

Winter Sunsets

Take me back to the winter sunsets
through the long unwinding roads
that carry the remains of the dusk to come.

The more you will talk concrete,

      the more I will slip away into abstract.

Isn't it...?

Isn't it difficult to look away, into an abyss,

when you are just passing by?

Isn't it difficult to keep on walking,

when you are nearing?

Isn't it difficult to grasp,

that now, you are so close yet so far?

Isn't it difficult to forget,

that we just crossed each other's path so unknowingly?

Isn't it difficult for once,

to not to turn and see how far each of us has gone?

Sitting by the Pavement

aisle of few stairs,

pavements soaked in tranquillity,

crossed hands, a few pages to sift through or maybe more,

heavy sighs,

no, maybe, they were turning light now,

sunlit breeze,

whirling thoughts

and pastel walls.

A look so vacant, they can't make anything of.

Serendipity

Tranquillity transcended
somewhat deliciously.
It was the time of winds
to whirl the serendipity.

Crimson

An aisle of crimson

swirled all along,

to bring closer

what was never near to the heart.

Animosity

The sealed utterances

quietened the anarchy.

To put down the agitation

that came through animosity.

83

Tell them, I fell in love with your pretty brown eyes.

Foreign Hostility

The bleak day

embraced foreign hostility,

brisk as ever

she held on to the brittle cold.

Laraib Zakir

Burn away

The ashes, burnt.
In a faraway land
Surreal as it could be.
I wished
The contemplations would burn along, too
The apprehension could vanish in the flickering flames
The inquisitiveness; devoured by the wildfire
And with them, the mere thought of you.

The facade you try to put up, I see through it every time.

Answers

It came all of a sudden,

an answer to their questioning glances.

Obvious as it was,

her resilience had them awed.

Abyss

The yearning had long gone

                     for everything that was once desired.

The eyes searched for an abyss

                     that lurked somewhere in the bottom.

89

Convictions

The convictions fragmented

into fabricated truths.

It was all about contentions

that were so firm.

I want my words to

I want to write something
which rips you apart.

I want my words
to whirl around your neck,
dance in the silver moonlight
and then strangle you,
so mercilessly that you drown in them.

I want my words
to pin you to the wall,
edge nearer, a little more
and whisper
a venomous lullaby in your ear.

I want my words
to hand you a sleek glass of red wine,
so divine,
that it cuts sharply through your throat
so that you forget to get drunk on them.

I want my words
to stab you
with a knife so lovingly,
repeatedly with your due compliance
so that you forget that you were supposed to bleed.

Laraib Zakir

I want my words
to drench you
in the wintry rain, that refuses to stop,
awfully running down into your bones
so that you ignite with nothing but blisters.

I want my words
to dress themselves in a silk gown
so elegantly, so unapologetically and walk down the aisle,
with black heels clicking so daringly on the sheer glass floor
to kiss you a bitter, cold death.

I want to write something
which rips you apart.

It should be well enough to disrupt your thoughts.

Laraib Zakir

Speculations

The sun rose

less threatening that day.

To ward off the perils

of captivating speculations.

Vulnerability

Vulnerability is treacherous
when I open up to you,
when I tell the slightest of anything about me.
You see,
I have cared for you,
maybe when I shouldn't have had,
because you won't remember any of it
in a few months to come
as we part our ways.

Chances are that you would forget me too.

—i really hope that the future proves me wrong.

It gets darker, the closer you get.

Ancient

Let's get lost in an ancient city
founded by the Romans—
let's dwell into London's nights.
Drink onto each other's sorrows
and wipe away the miseries.
Let's leave our scents as we walk through the
dark streets wrapped in secrets,
enter a timeworn café
and for once, have our silences speak for a lifetime.

There is nothingness in her eyes, for those who can't see.

Reminisces.

It's when you know
that you won't drown.
Although there is this void,

—but what remains, remains.

Laraib Zakir

Heal

It's when the calm settles.
after all that catastrophe,
the dreadful spells,
the venomous backdrops.
It's time to let go of
what stands in the way of healing.

It's them, waves.

I am the rumour, the waves bring.
Crashing, they tell you how stone-cold I have been.
Thrashing the shore with wrath,
they tell you how distraught my demeanour has been.
Whipping at the skies above,
they tell you I stare into nothingness.
Collapsing against the wild winds,
they tell you about the thorns I carry.
Defeating the horizons,
they tell you I walk away.
I am the rumour, the waves bring.

Not all damsels are in distress, some are the ones causing it.

Tonight

It's been so many nights.
Tonight, tell yourself some lies.
Better lies.
Put yourself to some sleep.

Laraib Zakir

Leap Year

The extra hours of this year,

might have just drowned themselves

in a sunset.

Silence

Silence is a beautiful revenge.
Isn't it?
With a tinge of eeriness
and then a whole lot of it,
it kills them.
First, slowly and steadily
and then out of drabness
it plunges its claws
into their conscience
and then withdraws.
leaving them agonised,
in pain, for many years to come.

Your Steps

The wind entwines the unknown,
tiptoes a light breeze,
I didn't know if it were you there,
but the steps, I hear them.

I wish our conversations never died, each time they did.

Nostalgia

There is something at the back of your mind.
You look afar and it all comes back.
But you, you stay there for a while,
because you want to.

Why?

Why is it
little moments of happiness
and
long nights filled with despair?

Have we grown ungrateful?

Or the melancholy that weighs the heart down
is heavier
than the delightedness which elates it?

Dusk/Dawn

There are times

When dusk meets dawn.

There,

Within you.

Wilderness

I stand at the coastline,
with the waves crashing at my feet and
the wilderness it brings
rages within
maybe a little more fiercely
when it's about you.

A question to the waves / that came and went by:

Is it with grief
that you return?
or
Is it with grief
that you leave?

Perhaps both.

But people.
They don't return.

Sunsets in the Capital

It's either in the descending hues

or the ascending leafless trees.

Laraib Zakir

Light

It takes time to see the light that creeps in,

that has always been there.

Through the window panes,

from behind the curtains,

past the wall creaks.

But maybe it has always been there.

Within you.

114

To stare at the ceiling or to go out in the night sky?

Laraib Zakir

A Walk, Together.

We were there,
at the same place.
But rarely did we,
ever walk together.

Forgiving

Is it wrong
that I have become
a little more forgiving?

The silence is still there,
not out of disregard
but because of letting it go.

Regrets

Regrets are remorseful.
leave them behind
for a while.

Obstructions

How I wish to defy
all the possibilities
                    for being there with you,
when you are there,
with everyone else.

Sky

Strewn is the sky
with stories
untold.

Emptiness

I look for you in the emptiness
because it was there,
I found you for the first time.

Fade away

To fade away
is not being fragile.
It is being brave enough
to drift away
from people's collective chaos
and create one for yourself.

I have been home to silence, stillness and reticence.

Laraib Zakir

Drizzle

And when it drizzles
Do you too sit back
and look outside?
Think to yourselves
about how you cannot, not love the rain?
It blurs everything beautifully
and you see things in pigmented specks.
A tinge of pink amidst clouds of green.
Do you too, somehow slither your finger
along with the raindrops
that go down the car's window?
Do you too cherish the pavements,
that lie enchanted,
drunk on the rain?

Wander

And we often wander off too far,
in search of something
that is never ours.

—but first, take a step back and return to yourselves.

Do you, too, like to stand under the pretty skies?

Decipher

take my words
and dissect them,
mourn them,
let them walk through a funeral and its rituals,
dig a grave and have them buried.

but before all that

—tell me one thing, have you ever read me?

Laraib Zakir

Subtle Wounds

And just like that, it started to happen.
Without knowing when
Everything grew weak.
The hair thinned, tangled in knots.
I walked, but the legs ached, way too much.
The fragile smiles failed to lighten up the pale face, it faded every
day.
The silence overtook, more than ever.
The pain seeped inside the bones, residing soulfully.
I traced the dark circles under the eyes, graver than ever.
Sleepless nights began to settle in, in hatred of my love for sleep.
At times I gasped for air; couldn't breathe.
I clenched at my ribs; they were crumbling sharply.
I could see more of those veins; tracing the path so clearly.
Paper cuts and a slight prick on the finger, oozed out crimson
profusely.
The tablets poured in, tasting awfully poisonous.
I wanted to scream out my lungs, once and for all.
Can a gush of fierce wind pierce through all the pain, just this one
time?
The sky must have seen something being taken away from those
green eyes, filling them with nothingness at last.
There, I was, perched against wounds.
Subtle wounds.
And just like that, it started to happen
Without knowing when
Everything grew weak.

September

May your September be light and crisp!

May the light breeze touch you from within

May you look forward to fall

May you forget what your heart can't

But you see,

It's better if you can hold on a little longer

To see if the cinders turn out to be in your favour

To see if the amber dusk brings you serenity

And to hold on enough

To live and die each day.

Laraib Zakir

November

And just as the sunlight slits through the window bars,

the sapphire fades into the

golden creases of what drapes the window.

It drizzles down the pane, to the eyes

and mixes the green with a tinge of hazel.

The fierceness, the wilderness;

all collapsed, reminisced and glorified

in that one sanctuary.

A speck of snowflake

melts into the clavicle, sinks deep into the skin,

and benumbs the conscious.

The pale, the faded, the silver,

all buried within.

By the last days, the winter breathes a sigh

and whispers a quelling spell.

Why is it that?

Why is it,
that when I'm no more,
you will come here more often?
Hesitate for a moment
and then sit there,
beside me as if I were there, too?

Why is it,
that you will dust off my rustic diary
and try to find your name inside?
But no, you wouldn't be able to.
Because, my dear,
You never learned to read between the lines, did you?

Why is it,
that you will walk towards my window,
open the curtains and look up at the sky
just like I did,
But the sky wouldn't be like that anymore.
Will you know then, that I always liked it dark?

Why is it,
that before picking up my vessel of dried flower petals,
you will stare long into it, into nothingness

and then get hold of a few, crumbling petals.
Feel them getting dusted off as you dearly hold them.
Will you then realize the fragility of life?

Why is it,
that you will sift through all my writings,
torn pieces of poetry, reckless scriptures of prose and wrecked
thoughts
and try to create meaning out of those.
But my dear,
Did chaos ever make sense to you?

Why is it,
that you never came to know,
it was you, all along
and then also, you weren't.
Maybe because there was everything
but, under the enchantment of oblivion.

Why is it,
that when I'm no more,
You will come here more often?

The pages,
they are still empty.
They utter your name
and I turn them over.

Acknowledgements

To my Dada; Muhammad Zaheer. You left us in 2019 and hold a piece of my heart. Your eyes, I can never forget, your voice, I shall never let go of. You always wanted to see me succeed. How highly you spoke of me to the others. How proud you always were of me! Until we meet again. Not only do I tremble when writing about you, but my heart also skips a beat each time it realizes you are no more among us.

To my brother; Muhammad Abbas. Watching you in pain and fight with it each day, gives me immeasurable strength. What you go through, seldom can imagine. I wish you, the best of health and happiness. Stay strong! Smile through like an Angel that you are!

To my Parents. Thank you, Papa, Muhammad Zakir. This book couldn't have been possible without you; your endless support and perpetual love for me. I will forever remain indebted for what you have continuously done for me, through thick and thin. Thank you, Mama, Malika Zakir. For the delicious food you always cook, how we shop together, and how you always suggest me an easy way out of all the problems that I encounter.

And to my mischievous brother; Muhammad Abdullah, the youngest. The one who tells me I do everything wrong, yet seeks my help for his homework.

Last but not the least, my proofreader and editor; Ateefah Sana Ur Rab, an amazing author herself. I pay my gratitude to you for your guidance through the difficult procedures and complexities, and for being there to help, whenever needed.

About the Author

Born in Islamabad and later raised in Lahore, Laraib has been moving between the two cities ever since.

There is one thing common to everything she thinks about and writes down, and that is this tinge of creativity. She believes words have the power of cutting through the sharpest emotions lingering in the heart, and those that fight their way to the mind. Immersed in novels, newspapers and magazines, Laraib found her interests at a very young age.

In second grade, she'd write tons of sentences in a day. Observing the growing passion, her father started to challenge her with new words every day and she'd scribble down her thoughts. Her interest advanced further with her participation in her school's creative essay and declamation competitions. In her O'Levels, she was appointed as the Student Correspondent for the school's Online News Portal.

Much of her work is now published in 'US-Magazine, The News International', beginning from the year 2017, including creative articles, short stories and poetry.

Laraib is known for weaving meaningful forms of prose and poetry, intended to create an impact. Her words resonate with the hassle taking place in the minds of people around the world.

Currently, she awaits the completion of her Bachelor's degree in Business Administration; with a Marketing Major.

@laraibzkir.23

@laraibzakir_

@Laraib_Sheikh

Chaos in Utter Silence

Copyright © 2020 by Laraib Zakir. All rights reserved. No part of this book may be used or reproduced in any manner whatsoever without the written permission of the author except for the use of brief quotations in context of book reviews.

ISBN: 978-969-23521-0-9

First Edition, November 2020.

Proofreader/Editor: Ateefah Sana Ur Rab

Cover Design by: Muhammad Asad Mir

www.ingramcontent.com/pod-product-compliance
Lightning Source LLC
Chambersburg PA
CBHW020720160726
47993CB00006B/2285